A Note to Parents and Caregivers:

Read-it! Readers are for children who are just starting on the amazing road to reading. These beautiful books support both the acquisition of reading skills and the love of books.

 The PURPLE LEVEL presents basic topics and objects using high frequency words and simple language patterns.

 The RED LEVEL presents familiar topics using common words and repeating sentence patterns.

 The BLUE LEVEL presents new ideas using a larger vocabulary and varied sentence structure.

 The YELLOW LEVEL presents more challenging ideas, a broad vocabulary, and wide variety in sentence structure.

 The GREEN LEVEL presents more complex ideas, an extended vocabulary range, and expanded language structures.

 The ORANGE LEVEL presents a wide range of ideas and concepts using challenging vocabulary and complex language structures.

When sharing a book with your child, read in short stretches, pausing often to talk about the pictures. Have your child turn the pages and point to the pictures and familiar words. And be sure to reread favorite stories or parts of stories.

There is no right or wrong way to share books with children. Find time to read with your child, and pass on the legacy of literacy.

Adria F. Klein, Ph.D.
Professor Emeritus
California State University
San Bernardino, California

For Tinkerpoon's fans Bill, Helena, Louis, and Nancy—J.K

Editors: Christianne Jones and Julie Gassman
Designer: Hilary Wacholz
Art Director: Heather Kindseth
The illustrations in this book were created with watercolor and pen.

Picture Window Books
151 Good Counsel Drive
P.O. Box 669
Mankato, MN 56002-0669
877-845-8392
www.picturewindowbooks.com

Printed in the United States of America.

All books published by Picture Window Books
are manufactured with paper containing at least
10 percent post-consumer waste.

Library of Congress Cataloging-in-Publication Data
Kalz, Jill.
Tuckerbean at the movies/by Jill Kalz; illustrated by Benton Mahan.
p. cm. — (Read-it! readers)
ISBN 978-1-4048-5231-0
[1. Motion pictures—Fiction. 2. Dogs—Fiction.] I. Mahan, Ben, ill. II. Title.
PZ7.K12655Tucj 2009
[E]—dc22
                                    2008030866

Tuckerbean
at the MOVIES

by Jill Kalz
illustrated by Benton Mahan

Special thanks to our reading adviser:

Adria F. Klein, Ph.D.
Professor Emeritus, California State University
San Bernardino, California

PICTURE WINDOW BOOKS
Minneapolis, Minnesota

On Saturdays, Peni has
music lessons.

She tells Tuckerbean to stay
in the house.

Sometimes Tuckerbean takes a nap. Sometimes he waves at cars. Today he walks around the corner and goes to the movies.

Tuckerbean watches airplanes fly over the fields. They rumble and roar.

Tuckerbean watches a princess fall in love. She hums a happy song.

Tuckerbean watches ghosts dive
and swoop. They give him
goose bumps.

Tuckerbean watches a big bear dance in a red dress. He giggles.

16

Tuckerbean watches basketball players jump high in the air. He claps and cheers.

When Peni is done with her lessons,
Tuckerbean is at the door.

Peni wrinkles her nose. "Why do you smell like popcorn?" she asks.

Tuckerbean likes all kinds of movies.

But he likes movies about
friends most of all.

More *Read-it!* Readers

Bright pictures and fun stories help you practice your reading skills. Look for more books at your level.

Benny and the Birthday Gift	*Pony Party*
The Best Lunch	*Princess Bella's Birthday Cake*
The Boy Who Loved Trains	*The Princesses' Lucky Day*
Car Shopping	*Rudy Helps Out*
Clinks the Robot	*The Sand Witch*
Firefly Summer	*Say "Cheese"!*
The Flying Fish	*The Snow Dance*
Gabe's Grocery List	*The Ticket*
Loop, Swoop, and Pull!	*Tuckerbean at Waggle World*
Patrick's Super Socks	*Tuckerbean in the Kitchen*
Paulette's Friend	*Wyatt and the Duck*

On the Web

FactHound offers a safe, fun way to find Web sites related to topics in this book. All of the sites on FactHound have been researched by our staff.

1. Visit *www.facthound.com*

2. Type in this special code:
   140485231X

3. Click on the FETCH IT button.

Your trusty FactHound will fetch the best sites for you! A complete list of *Read-it!* Readers is available on our Web site:
www.picturewindowbooks.com